Books should be returned on or before the
last date stamped below

0 7 MAR 2018

18 MAY 2017
HQ

1 1 JUN 2018

-5 JUN 2019

1 3 OCT 20

2 9 AUG 2019

1 7 JUN 2017

2 1 NOV 2018

-3 SEP 2019

-7 NOV 2019

2 7 MAR 2019

0 7 SEP 2017

0 7 DEC 2019

1 0 MAY 2019

2 3 SEP 2017

1 0 AUG 2019

1 8 JAN 2020

1 3 OCT 2017

2 2 FEB 2020

D0230115

For lightness of being…

First published 2005 by Walker Books Ltd
87 Vauxhall Walk, London SE11 5HJ

2 4 6 8 10 9 7 5 3 1

© 2005 Kim Lewis Ltd

The right of Kim Lewis to be identified as
author/illustrator of this work has been asserted by
her in accordance with the Copyright, Designs
and Patents Act 1988

This book has been typeset in Berling

Printed in Singapore

British Library Cataloguing in Publication Data:
a catalogue record for this book is available
from the British Library

ISBN 0-7445-8698-4

www.walkerbooks.co.uk

Here We Go, Harry

Kim Lewis

WALKER BOOKS
AND SUBSIDIARIES

LONDON · BOSTON · SYDNEY · AUCKLAND

There was a little hill near Harry's house.

It wasn't too high. It wasn't too far.

Harry climbed up with his friends, Ted and Lulu.

On the top of the hill it was windy.

Clouds were floating along in the sky.

Birds were swooping up and down in the air.

"Whoops!" said Harry, as the breeze flapped his ears.

"Wheee!" said Ted, as it tickled his fur.

"Whoopee!" said Lulu, feeling loopy and frisky.

Lulu ran in the grass.

She hopped one, two, three.

She leapt in the wind from the hill.

"Look at me, Ted and Harry!" called Lulu.

And she flew in the air as light as could be.

"Wait for me, Lulu!" said Ted.

He ran in the grass. He hopped one, two, three.

"Wheee! Look at me!" cried Ted.

In the breeze from the hill Ted flew in the air.

"Whoopee!" and "Wheee!" went Lulu and Ted,
as they tumbled down the hill in the soft summer grass.
They went roly poly all the way to the bottom.
"What about me?" wondered Harry.

Harry peered over the edge of the hill.

His ears flapped this way and that in the wind.

His fur felt ruffled.

His trunk felt tickled.

"Come on, Harry!" called Lulu and Ted.

Harry ran back a little.

He hopped ... one, two, three.

Then a small puff of wind blew Harry's ears.

Both of them flapped right over his eyes.

Harry stopped on the edge of the hill.

He couldn't take off.

He didn't feel right.

He didn't feel loopy,

or swoopy, or light.

"You can do it, Harry!" called Lulu and Ted.

But Harry just sat there, all by himself.

Lulu and Ted ran back up the hill.

"We'll go with you, Harry," said Ted.

"Ready now, Harry?" said Lulu.

Lulu and Ted held Harry's ears.

They ran in the grass.

They hopped … one, two, three.

"Oh, OH!" said Harry. He took a deep breath.

And before Harry knew it, off they all flew.

His ears spread wide in the wind.

He felt as loopy and swoopy and light as could be,

for one long, lovely second.

Then the three little friends landed tumble-slump
and went roly poly in the soft hill grass.
"Whoopee! Wheee! Whoops!" cried Lulu, Ted and Harry.
"We did it," said Harry. "We did it together!"

And on the little hill near Harry's house,

which wasn't too high and wasn't too far,

Harry, Ted and Lulu went jumping again.

"Here we go, Harry!" said Lulu and Ted.

And Harry, with his ears spread wide in the wind,

flew the longest and lightest of all.